TAR BEACH

TAR BEACH
· Arthur Getz ·
The Dial Press 🦁 New York

Published by
The Dial Press
1 Dag Hammarskjold Plaza
New York, New York 10017

Copyright © 1979 by Arthur Getz
All rights reserved. Manufactured in the U.S.A.
First Printing
Typography by Denise Cronin Neary

Library of Congress Cataloging in Publication Data
Getz, Arthur. Tar Beach.
Summary: Joey and his sister, Teresa, find that
rooftops make wonderful beaches on hot summer days.
[1. Apartment houses—Fiction. 2. City and
town life—Fiction] I. Title.
PZ7.G3298Tar   [E]   78-72198
ISBN 0-8037-8521-6
ISBN 0-8037-8522-4 lib. bdg.

*The art for each picture consists of a black line drawing
and three halftone separations.*

To Frances Goldin

The sun woke me up—it's already hot. Last night was so hot, Teresa and I slept on the fire escape.

I give her legs a push. "Get your feet off my stomach. You're squashing me."

Boy hears us and jumps out the window, wagging his tail. He starts to lick my face.

"Go away, stop licking me!" I shout.

"Quiet out there!" Pop calls from the bedroom.

"Joey pushed me."

"Quiet, the both of you!"

Boy goes back to the kitchen. I can see him drinking his water under the sink. *Slurp. Slurp. Slurp.* Boy is hot too.

Saturday is the best day of the week because Mom and Pop are home from work.

We go shopping right after breakfast. Our carts fold up when they're empty. It's fun pushing the carts, but you have to watch out not to bump into people on the street.

"Good morning, Mrs. Broda," Mom says.

"Hot enough for you, Tom?" asks Pop.

"Hi, Pepe," I call. "Pepe's in my class, Pop."

Teresa sees two friends, but she's busy steering her shopping cart.

The supermarket is air-conditioned. It's nice and cool. Mom gets out her grocery list: bananas, carrots, mustard, pickles, Brillo, shoe polish, and lots lots more.

"Don't forget chewing gum, Mom," Teresa tells her. "And cookies."

"And watermelon!" I shout.

Then we go back home. The hard part is pulling the heavy shopping carts up the stairs. Mom and Pop do the work. Teresa and I help.

Mom brings the food into the kitchen to put in the refrigerator so nothing spoils. Then we have some watermelon.

"We're going downstairs to play," I tell Mom.

"Stay on the block," Mom says.

She sticks her head out the window and watches until Teresa and I are on the street and she sees who we're going to play with. Teresa looks up and waves.

"Look out for cars, Teresa," Mom calls.

Our street is closed off so no cars can drive through. Kids play all over the street—every kind of game. Old people sit on the stoops and watch.

"Let's run upstairs and get our bathing suits," I say to Teresa. We put them on fast and run out again. The street is hot. It hurts bare feet.

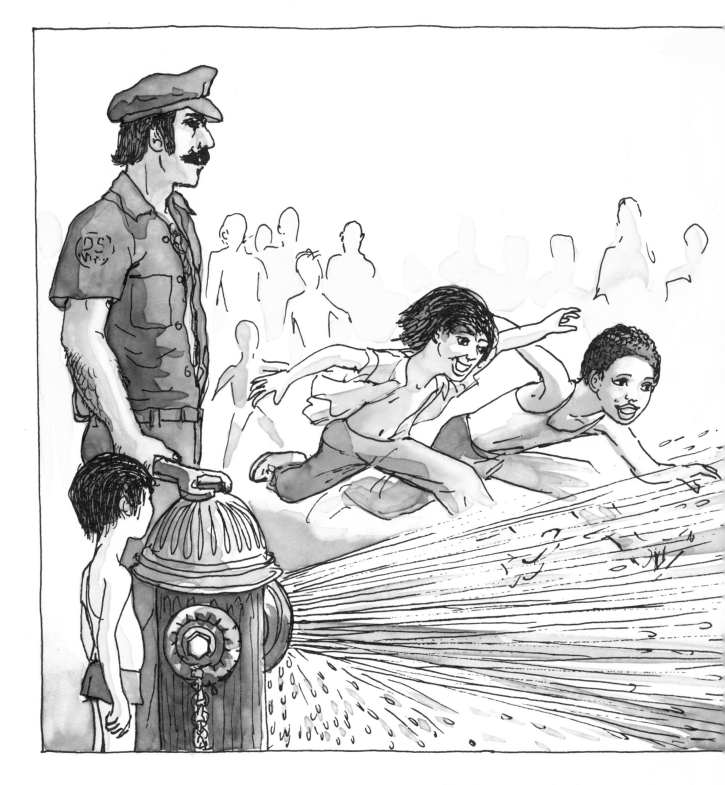

The best thing is when they open the fire hydrant. A giant spray of water shoots out across the street. Big kids jump right in with their clothes on. Later the smaller ones get in too. Everyone screams. The water's like ice.

"Watch me, watch me," I shout. I stand in the water spray and walk backward to see how close to the hydrant I can get before I yell "Ouch!" and run away.

Pepe does it next. His mother shouts "*Bravo*!" That means well done in Spanish.

Little kids follow the water along the gutter until it goes down
the sewer. They make boats out of empty cans and milk cartons.

Time for lunch. I ring the front doorbell. Pepe and his sister come too. Mom buzzes, and Teresa opens the door.

We all dry off, but Boy shakes himself and sprays us with water again.

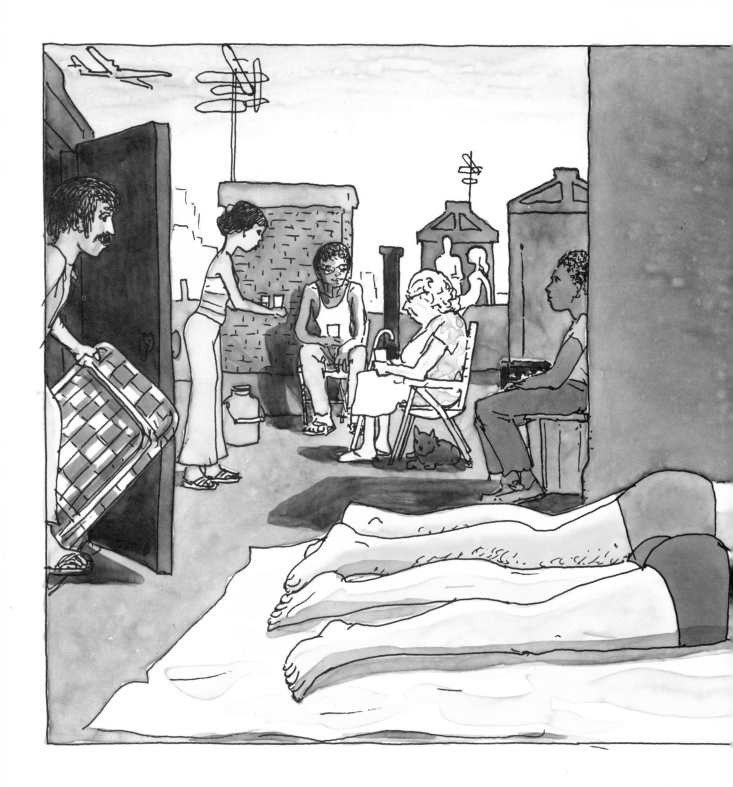

After lunch we go up to the roof. People call it Tar Beach. We all relax up there and take off our shirts to get a tan. Sometimes there's a breeze.

Pop goes downstairs when the baseball game starts.

"Why don't you stay here where it's cool?" Mom asks, but Pop likes to watch the game on TV.

Pedro's ma has a big Thermos of lemonade with ice. She gives everyone some.

We have a big water-pistol fight. Then we see the pigeons coming.
Henry says, "Let's go to Sal's."

Henry leads the way. We climb from one roof to the next all the
way to the roof where Sal keeps his pigeons.

Sal is watering his tomatoes. "Okay, come on," he says.

Sal used to be a prizefighter. Now he takes care of the building
and fixes things. He has a hundred keys on a chain. Sal lives all
alone in a little house on the roof. He keeps racing pigeons up there.

Sal has a punching bag that he hits every day.

All the kids like Sal. Pancho says he killed a man once. We stay and talk to him and watch what he does. "There's going to be a thunderstorm this afternoon," Sal says.

Ding-ding-ding. The Mr. Softee truck!

"So long, Sal," we yell.

We run back to ask for nickels, dimes, and quarters. Then we rush out to get in line. Finally all the kids get their ice cream.

The Mr. Softee man lights his cigar and looks up and down the street. He rings the bell again and again, but it's time to move on. We've spent all our money.

The sun is going behind some clouds. It's getting dark and the wind is blowing. Paper bags fly and lids of garbage cans bang around.

Mrs. Zaccaro gets up. "I'm going to close my windows."

Mrs. Feldman remembers that she has wash on the line and leaves. We hear the *squeak-squeak* of the rusty pulley as she pulls on her line, taking in the wash.

Suddenly the rain splashes down. Kids run to the doorways. Then it
pours buckets. Thunder roars, and Teresa and I start shivering.

When the rain stops, everyone runs out again, splashing in the gutters. The rain cooled everything off. The city looks washed clean. Tonight will be cool, and we'll all sleep well.

But now—it's time for supper.